Nature Stories

Bella: A Butterfly's Story

Joanne Randolph

alphabet soup™
an imprint of

WINDMILL BOOKS™
New York

For Hannah, who loves bugs, from butterflies to beetles

Published in 2009 by Windmill Books, LLC
303 Park Avenue South, Suite # 1280, New York, NY 10010-3657

First Edition

Book Design and Illustrations by: Planman Technologies (India) Pvt. Ltd.

Publisher Cataloging Data

Randolph, Joanne
      Bella : a butterfly's story / by Joanne Randolph.
p.   cm. – (Nature stories)
Summary: Bella tells how she and her brothers and sisters were once wormy caterpillars but turned into beautiful Monarch butterflies.
ISBN 978-1-60754-098-4 (lib.) – ISBN 978-1-60754-099-1 (pbk.)
ISBN 978-1-60754-100-4 (6-pack)
      1. Monarch butterfly—Juvenile fiction   [1. Monarch butterfly—Fiction
2. Butterflies—Fiction   3. Caterpillars—Fiction   4. Metamorphosis—Fiction]
I. Title   II. Series
      [E]—dc22

Manufactured in the United States of America

Hi, there. My name is Bella. I am a butterfly. Don't worry, I'm not sticking my tongue out at you. Really, I was just taking a drink from this tasty flower.

I use my long tongue like a straw to drink a sweet juice called nectar from inside flowers. Nectar is my favorite drink. What's your favorite drink?

I may not seem big to you, but I am actually one of the biggest butterflies in the world. I am a monarch. My aunts, uncles, and cousins live in places around the world, from the United States all the way to Australia.

My mom looks just like me, now that I am not a baby anymore.
We both have orange and black markings all over our wings.
My dad looks pretty much the same, too, but he has an extra
spot on his wings and he is a little bigger than Mom and I.

We butterflies are different from all other insects, or bugs. We have scales covering our beautiful wings! Our scales are like the little plates that cover a snake's body. These scales help create some of the beautiful colors and patterns we have on our wings. Pretty fancy, don't you think?

11

I wasn't always this fancy. I started out as a small egg. My mom laid me and my brothers and sisters on a milkweed plant. After about four days, we broke free from the eggs.

We were worm-like creatures called caterpillars when we came out of our eggs. My brothers thought that was really cool. My sisters and I looked forward to growing into something more beautiful.

For about two weeks, my brothers, sisters, and I ate lots of milkweed. Mom told us to eat as much as we could because it would give us energy. Have you ever planned for a big day or trip? You may have packed a lunch, extra clothes, or your toothbrush. That's kind of like what we were doing. We were packing up lots of food so we would be ready for what came next for us.

We stopped feeding and picked a nice leaf. We started spinning a pad. Each of us attached our pupa, or chrysalis, to the pad. Those are just big words for the nice, cozy beds we made for ourselves.

I stayed in my chrysalis for about two weeks. Then I poked my way out. My brothers and sisters did, too. No more caterpillars for us. We were beautiful butterflies! We stretched our wings, let them dry, and then we were ready to fly. My mom said she was very proud of us. And we felt proud of ourselves. I bet you have done things you were proud of, too. It's a great feeling, isn't it?

Well, I'm off to find some flowers. My job as a butterfly is to float from flower to flower, drinking nectar. That's how I'll spend most of my life. So when you go by a flower, take a closer look. If you see me or someone from my monarch family, make sure to say "Hello!"

For more great fiction and nonfiction,
go to windmillbooks.com.